Bumble Bear

THE GARDEN PARTY

WRITTEN BY JAMES HOFFMAN
ILLUSTRATED BY JOHN SANFORD
EDITED BY SHANNON M. MULLALLY, Ph.D.

Bumble Bear loved honey. But despite scheme after scheme and plan after plan, the honey shelves in his cottage were empty. His wife, Gwendolyn, and his cubs, Wear and Tear, often smiled to themselves over his bumbling efforts to get honey for the shelves.

One morning at breakfast, Bumble Bear sat staring into an empty honey jar.

Gwendolyn was looking out the window when she turned and said to Wear and Tear, "Today you can help me plant flowers in my garden."
"I thought you already planted strawberries!" said Tear.
"I thought you planted raspberries, too!" said Wear.
"I did," said Gwendolyn. "But the berry blossoms need to be pollinated. If I plant a lot of flowers, the bees will come and give us their help."

Bumble Bear's head snapped up. "Bees?" he said. "Bees!" he continued thinking. "Where bees *are*, honey *is*! Right here on Honey Hill Farm!" A plan formed in his honey-track mind. "I'll plant my *own* garden," he mumbled. "The bees will love *me*. They'll *thank* me, too—with honey!" He smiled as he thought of eating honey all day long.

That day, Wear and Tear and Gwendolyn Bear began working in the garden, patiently planting flowers. Gwendolyn made Bumble Bear work, too. He dug and hoed under the hot sun. "Gardens are a lot of work," he grumbled. "There *must* be an easier way!"

As the sun set, Gwendolyn said to her cubs, "Thank you for all your help today. This garden will be as pretty as a *picture*." At that moment, Bumble Bear stumbled onto another sweet idea. "Pictures!" he thought.

Back in his study, Bumble Bear worked feverishly with his paints. He painted a *wild* flower, *one* flower, which took him a very long time. "There *must* be an easier way!" he thought. Then he smiled and got a stack of Gwendolyn's gardening magazines. His scissors flew until he had a stack of brightly colored flower pictures. He sang to himself,

"Pretty as a picture...ta dee, ta dum!"

When morning came, Bumble Bear nailed all of his flower pictures on sticks. There were pictures of sunflowers, roses, peonies, marigolds and even orchids that would be set around his painted masterpiece, the *wild* wildflower. "These will bloom all summer long," he thought as he worked. "I'll never have to work in my garden again, and the bees will love them!"

Bumble Bear carried the flower pictures out to his garden and planted them. He plucked the red and blue silk flowers from several vases Gwendolyn had in the house and planted them, too. The bright jumble of flowers could be seen from far away.

All that summer, Wear and Tear and Gwendolyn Bear
hoed and tilled, weeded and watered. Bumble Bear
spent his time lying in the shade, listening to the
hum of the bees, and dreaming his honey dreams.
"It seems like there are more bees in the garden
than ever," he thought happily. He watched
the bees as they hovered around
his garden, looking at the pictures
before flying over to Gwendolyn's
garden to continue their
pollination work.

Some days, Bumble Bear would tiptoe down to the beehive, which was bursting with honey. Honey dripped down the sides, and Bumble Bear would cautiously lick a little off. "Delicious!" he said. "They are working extra hard thanks to my inspiration."

One evening, Gwendolyn showed Bumble Bear a tiny invitation sealed with beeswax. "The bees are having a garden party tomorrow," said Gwendolyn. "They have invited us and wish to thank us for our hard work this summer." "At last!" thought Bumble Bear.

That night, Bumble Bear had sweet dreams of honey by the pot, by the barrel, by the wagonload—his honey due for a job well done.

The next day, the whole Bear family dressed in flowery finery to attend the bees' garden party. The hive was beautifully decorated, and the meadow was filled with harmonious buzzing as the bees waited for their honored guests. Gwendolyn Bear received a flower vase that the bees had filled with honey, and Wear and Tear were given a shiny bucket holding a large honey comb.

Then it was Bumble Bear's turn. He stepped up, beaming to receive his sweet reward. The bees flew to him, humming humorously now, and placed a picture of a honey jar into his anxiously awaiting paws. Bumble Bear looked very sadly at the picture, a symbol for *real* honey. His stomach grumbled, and his honey hopes crumbled. Gwendolyn Bear smiled gently and said, "A very pretty *picture* of honey, don't you think?"

That night, Bumble Bear locked himself in his study, thinking and planning, with the picture of the honey jar propped up in front of him. "One of these days, I'll stumble onto something. I'll come up with a *picture* perfect plan. What if..."